FROGNAPPED

ALSO BY
ANGIE SAGE

·3·
ARAMINTA SPOOKIE

FROGNAPPED

as told to
ANGIE SAGE

illustrated by
JIMMY PICKERING

KATHERINE TEGEN BOOKS
An Imprint of HarperCollins*Publishers*

Araminta Spookie 3: Frognapped

Text copyright © 2007 by Angie Sage

Illustrations copyright © 2007 by Jimmy Pickering

Library of Congress Cataloging-in-Publication Data

Sage, Angie.

    Frognapped / as told to Angie Sage ; illustrated by Jimmy
Pickering. — 1st ed.

        p.   cm.

    "Araminta Spookie 3."

    Summary: Barry Wizzard's five acrobatic frogs are missing, and
Araminta and her best friend, Wanda, aided by the spectral Sir
Horace, follow the trail to Morris's Water Wonderland, where
something fishy is going on.

    ISBN-13: 978-0-06-077487-5 (trade bdg.)

    ISBN-10: 0-06-077487-8 (trade bdg.)

    ISBN-13: 978-0-06-077488-2 (lib. bdg.)

    ISBN-10: 0-06-077488-6 (lib. bdg.)

    [1. Ghosts—Fiction. 2. Lost and found possessions—Fiction. 3.
Frogs—Fiction. 4. Mystery and detective stories.] I. Pickering,
Jimmy, ill. II. Title.

PZ7.S13035Fro 2006   2006030535

[Fic]—dc22   CIP

                                                              AC

Typography by Amy Ryan

1 2 3 4 5 6 7 8 9 10

First Edition

For Katy, Lizzy,
and Laura, with love

CONTENTS

FROGNAPPED

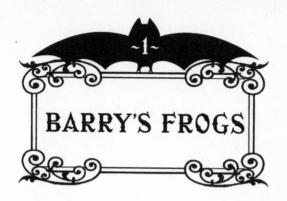

BARRY'S FROGS

"Araminta, where have you put my frogs?"
What kind of question is that? But last week that is exactly what Barry Wizzard asked me.

I did not answer.

I did not answer because when someone in Spookie House has lost something they always say, "Araminta, where have you put my . . . ?" You can fill in the blank with anything you like

and chances are, someone will have thought that I put it somewhere. I do not know why.

Take yesterday, for instance. Wanda Wizzard, who lives with me in Spookie House—along with her parents, Barry and Brenda, and my aunt Tabitha and uncle Drac—asked me where I had put her green socks. Wanda is supposed to be my best friend, although you'd never believe it from the way she talks to me. So I asked Wanda why she thought I would want to even *touch* her smelly old green socks, let alone put them somewhere, and she just smiled the irritating smile that she has learned from my aunt Tabby and said, "How do *I* know, Araminta?" So I told her they were in the compost heap at the bottom of the garden. She came back hours later with eggshells and moldy carrot tops in her hair and she didn't ask again.

But Barry did ask again. "Araminta," he said, sounding snappy.

"Yes, Barry?" I replied politely, even though I just knew what he was going to say. Which he did.

"Where have you *put my frogs?*"

It was very trying. Wanda and I were busy, we had things to do. Wanda was building a house to put some small spiders in so they did not get eaten by the big spiders. And because that was unfair to the big spiders, I was building a house for *them*. Building a spider house is not easy, but Barry did not care because Barry thinks only about his frogs. They are acrobatic frogs, which means they do lots of tricks, like jumping over each other and turning cartwheels.

And, they can do a frog pyramid, which I guess is all right if you like that sort of thing. Barry has—or rather Barry *had*—five frogs, and he had names for them all, but I can't remember them as they were silly frog names like Ermintrude and Gonzilla.

Barry stood right in front of me, tapping his pointy blue shoes like he was waiting for someone who was late. "It's not funny anymore, Araminta," he said.

I finished gluing the roof onto the spider house and then I made sure that I looked like I was thinking very carefully about what Barry had said. "I did not think it was funny in the first place actually, Barry," I said. "I have better things to do than put a bunch of stupid frogs *anywhere*."

"You haven't put them in the bath again

and let the water out, have you, Araminta?" he asked.

"No, I haven't. Anyway, it wasn't I who took the plug out. It was Aunt Tabby. I was just giving them a nice swim."

"The water was hot, Araminta."

"I was only trying to warm them up. They looked cold."

"They looked even colder when I fished them out of the drain, Araminta."

Have you noticed that when someone is annoyed with you they keep on saying your whole name? It is a real giveaway. Aunt Tabby can say as many times as she likes, "No, I am not annoyed with you, Araminta, I am just disappointed, that is all." But I know she is annoyed because of the "Araminta" part. My uncle Drac always calls me Minty and he is never annoyed with me, so that proves it.

I could see that Barry was not going to believe me about the frogs, so when Wanda said, "We'll go and look for them if you like, Dad. Won't we, Araminta?" I thought I had better say "Yes, Wanda" and smile like I was very keen to do it.

Barry and Wanda both looked at me in a suspicious way, but there is no pleasing some people.

Spookie House is a huge house. I do not know how many rooms there are because whenever I start counting I am sure that some of them move around, just to annoy me, so that I either count them twice or not at all. Then there are the secret rooms, and I only know one of those, because obviously the rest of them are secret. The secret room that I do know is in the middle of the house at the end of a secret tunnel and it belongs to Sir Horace, who is one of our ghosts.

So you can see that it was not easy to look for frogs in such a big place. Plus lots of the rooms are full of what Uncle Drac calls junk, but what Aunt Tabby calls "finds"—which means she has found a bunch of old furniture, I do not know where. Then you can add the piles of spiderwebs that are stuffed full of enormous spiders, which could probably eat all Barry's frogs for breakfast and still be hungry, and you can see that I did not expect to find any of Barry's frogs in Spookie House.

I was right. We didn't.

But we did find:

- one Wellington boot with a family of mice living in it
- one elephant's-foot doorstop (I do not know where the rest of the elephant was)
- six pairs of Aunt Tabby's spectacles huddling together in a dark corner behind some moldy curtains on the landing, hoping not to be found
- one crate of odd knitting needles
- five bolts from Sir Horace's helmet

And then Aunt Tabby found *us*.

My aunt Tabby is always creeping around the house trying to catch me and Wanda doing something that she thinks we shouldn't. But she didn't have to creep around to find us this time, because Wanda was yelling so loudly that it was a bit of a giveaway.

We were right at the top of the house in a little turret opposite Uncle Drac's bat turret. Wanda had a telescope that Brenda and Barry had given her for her birthday, and I thought it would be a good place to go to look for the frogs because you can see for miles out the window. But it is hard it see frogs, even through a telescope. So I told Wanda that she might see more if she climbed on top of one of Aunt Tabby's finds—a horrible old wardrobe right by the window. Wanda is not very good at climbing, but I helped her up, and I was just about to pass her the telescope when there was a loud *crack* and she disappeared. Well, most of her did. I could still see her head sticking out, which looked quite funny, although Wanda didn't seem to think so.

Then she started yelling. When Wanda yells you have to put your fingers in your ears or your eardrums will explode.

"Be quiet, Wanda," I told her. "You'll frighten the frogs if they're here. Then they'll all hop off and we'll never find them."

"I don't care about the stupid frogs," Wanda yelled. "Get me out of here!"

I was shocked. "Wanda," I said, "Barry would be very upset to hear you call his frogs stupid."

"Well, you do all the time. Get me *out*! Help, help!" Suddenly there was a thump and Wanda's head disappeared. Now she was right inside the wardrobe.

"Help!" yelled Wanda. "*Heeelp!*"

I tried to open the door, but it was locked and there was no key. I pulled on the door handle and it came right off in my hand.

In between Wanda's yells I could hear Aunt Tabby's footsteps clattering up the stairs from the hall and then thumping up the winding backstairs to the little room in the turret roof. She threw open the door and a hat stand fell over and landed on her foot. Aunt Tabby did not look pleased. Her hair was sticking up like it does when she is mad and her spectacles were about to make a break for freedom and join their friends by the moldy curtains on the landing.

"What *are* you doing in here, Araminta?" she said.

"Wanda's in here too," I told her, because I am tired of always getting the blame.

"Where?" asked Aunt Tabby suspiciously.

"In the wardrobe."

"Help!" shouted Wanda, sounding kind of muffled.

Aunt Tabby sighed. "Brenda!" she yelled out the door. "Brendaaaa. Wanda's stuck again."

It took forever to get Wanda out. In the end Aunt Tabby had to get her crowbar to open the wardrobe door. She was not happy because the door split in two. Brenda was not pleased either, because when Wanda fell out of the wardrobe she was covered in dust and had scraped her knees. And they both blamed *me*.

We had to promise never, ever to climb on wardrobes again, even though I pointed out that I never had, so if I did, it would not be *again*, it would be for the first time. Aunt Tabby was just about to say something when the doorbell rang downstairs and Brenda and Aunt Tabby both rushed off to get it. Aunt Tabby always likes to be the first one to answer the door because she is so nosy, but Brenda, who is just as nosy, is a surprisingly fast runner and can beat Aunt Tabby down the stairs any day.

Wanda and I listened to their footsteps disappearing. I waited for Wanda to start moaning at me, but she didn't "While I was in the wardrobe I was thinking," she said.

"No you weren't, you were yelling," I pointed out.

"Actually, Araminta, it is perfectly possible to yell and think at the same time," Wanda said sniffily. "I was thinking about the frogs. Now I know what's happened to them."

I didn't get it. "How? Have they written a note and left it in the wardrobe?"

Wanda sighed like she was pretending to be patient. "Frogs can't write, Araminta. But they do leave clues. Little sticky frog footprints. And have we seen any?"

I shook my head.

"Exactly," said Wanda, sounding like she was some kind of detective. "Which can mean only one thing."

"Can it?" I asked.

Wanda glanced around as if she was expecting Aunt Tabby to jump out from one of the other horrible wardrobes. Then she whispered, "Dad's frogs have been *frog-napped*."

~2~
THE SPOOKIE
DETECTIVE AGENCY

"'Frognapping' is not a proper word," I told Wanda.

"It should be," said Wanda, "because that's what's happened to Dad's frogs."

We were sitting on the back steps, keeping out of the way of Aunt Tabby, who was still annoyed, and also out of the way of Uncle Drac, who was being taken for a walk around the hall by the nurse. Uncle Drac broke both

his legs not long ago. They are all right now, but he has to learn to walk properly again, which he does not like, as he would rather sit and knit. But Aunt Tabby does not believe that anyone should sit down for long, especially if they are doing something they like, so she found a nurse to come and make him walk.

I was thinking hard. "If something has been frognapped," I said, "then there has to be a frognapper. And we will have to find him . . . or her."

"But how?" asked Wanda.

"Easy," I told her. "We shall have to become detectives."

"Wow," said Wanda, sounding excited. "How do we do that?"

"I shall start up the Spookie Detective Agency. I shall be chief detective and you can

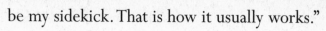

be my sidekick. That is how it usually works."

Wanda did not look as pleased as she should have been. "But *I* want to be chief detective," she said. "Of the Wizzard Detective Agency."

"You can't have two detective agencies working on the same case," I told her. "It just leads to trouble. Oh look, here's Uncle Drac. Hello, Uncle Drac!"

I could see the sunlight shining on Uncle Drac's round, pale face as he slowly came toward us along the passageway that led out of the hall. I was really happy to see him. Of course I always am, but this time I was especially happy because I could tell that Wanda was not finished talking about detective agencies. But as Uncle Drac shuffled nearer I could see that he did not look happy to see me. In fact, he did not look happy at all.

"Oh. Hello, Minty," he mumbled. He tried to smile, but it didn't really work. Usually Uncle Drac has a really big smile and you can see his lovely long, pointy teeth at the far corners of his mouth, but this was a no-teeth smile with his mouth turned down. But I did not take it personally because following right behind him I could see the reason for his no-teeth smile: Nurse Watkins.

Nurse Watkins was *big*. It is not that I am not used to big—Brenda, who is Wanda's mom, is also big but in a soft and squashy kind of way. If you hug Brenda it feels like you have dived into a great big feather pillow smelling of lavender, which is nice. It is in fact a lot nicer than hugging Aunt Tabby, who is okay and tries her best, but her elbows always get in the way and she smells of soap. You would not want to hug Nurse Watkins though. It would be dangerous because of all those muscles. Nurse Watkins has big muscled arms and legs, which Uncle Drac says is because she is really a wrestler. The previous morning when Nurse Watkins had arrived and Brenda was trying to find Uncle Drac, I had to sit and talk to

her forever. I asked her all kinds of questions about wrestling, like what were the best head-locks she had ever made and did she have to train every day and stuff like that, and she just stared at me in a really weird way. Uncle Drac was pleased though, because by the time Brenda had found him (in his hedge hideaway) Nurse Watkins had gone.

But today Nurse Watkins had not gone. She was there, muscles and all, right behind Uncle Drac. "*Left* foot up and lift and step. *Right* foot up and lift and step. *Don't shuffle.* Keep those knees straight. Knees, Drac, *knees!*" Nurse Watkins's voice boomed down the passage, bounced off the step, and hurt my ears. "Put a bit of *effort* in. *Left* foot up and lift and step. *Right* foot up and lift and step. One-two, one-two. One-two-*one*. Oh come on, Drac, anyone would think you were on your way to a funeral."

"It'll be my own funeral at this rate," I heard Uncle Drac growl, although I don't think Nurse Watkins did, as she just kept right on going. "*Left* foot up and lift and step. *Right* foot up and lift and step. *Knees!*"

I decided Uncle Drac needed rescuing.

What I find works really well as a general diversion is the help-me-I'm-choking face. Well, it's more than just a face really; for maximum effect it is best to do the sound effects and the actions too. I will pass on the tip, as you never know when it might come in handy:

STEP 1: Grab your throat with one hand. I used to use two hands but have recently found that waving the other hand frantically in the air and making clawing shapes with your fingers is much more effective.

STEP 2: Stare hard at your eyebrows so that your eyes roll up to the top of your head as far as they will go. Wanda says mine go a long way and you can see a lot of white. The more white of your eyes people can see, the better. I do not know why, but it bothers them.

STEP 3: Stagger. The easiest way is to lean over to one side—the opposite side to the arm-waving one is best—and then run in zigzags. It is best to vary your speed, and you can also put in a couple of sudden stops to spice it up. If you do stop, try leaning forward and really going for the choking noises at the same time. It's probably best to leave this toward the end, though, for the best result.

STEP 4: Sound effects. Choking noises (see above) are easy to do. I am quite good at doing them in the back of my throat now, although it can make your throat a bit sore afterward if you really go for it. Coughing is good too, and wheezing if you can manage it. The most successful method is to really get going on the sound effects and then, when you have got everyone's attention, you suddenly stop and continue with just the actions.

STEP 5: The silent gasping stage (see above). Wait until you have acquired your full available audience, as this is very effective. For best effect do the silent gasping while running around in small circles.

STEP 6: Now exit before people get bored and/or suspicious. Stop dead and give a small, polite cough. Smile, say, "Ooh, that's better," and walk away. It is best not to bow. I did that once and it gave the game away.

So now you know how I rescued Uncle Drac—or tried to, as it didn't quite work out that way. You see, I forgot that I was doing the choking act in front of a *nurse*.

Anyway, I put Step 1 into action right away and headed for Uncle Drac. He looked a bit surprised as I ran toward him, but I rushed past (as I did not want to worry him), and as

I squeezed by Nurse Watkins I got going on Steps 2 and 3 big-time. Then I headed off toward the hall. I was really getting into it now, and I could hear Nurse Watkins's heavy boots thumping down the passageway after me. Good, I thought, it's worked—now Uncle Drac can escape.

I was well into Step 4 and about to embark on Step 5 when I was grabbed from behind by Nurse Watkins. She wrapped her wrestler's forearms around my waist and gave a great heave. I thought I was going to explode.

For once, Aunt Tabby came to my rescue. "What are you *doing?*" she yelled at Nurse Watkins.

"Heimlich maneuver!" Nurse Watkins yelled back.

Then Uncle Drac arrived. "Minty, Minty!"

he shouted. "Cough it up, Minty."

Needless to say, I did not get to Step 5. Aunt Tabby, who is stronger than you might think, wrestled me from Nurse Watkins's grasp. "She's fine," Aunt Tabby told her very firmly. "There is no need for such a fuss; Araminta often does this."

"Well, you ought to get her checked out,"

said Nurse Watkins, sounding annoyed at having had her prey dragged from her claws. Aunt Tabby made me sit down on the horrible monster chair by the hall clock, and I found myself surrounded by Aunt Tabby, Brenda, Barry, Uncle Drac, Wanda, and Nurse Watkins, all staring at me.

I managed a weak smile and coughed a bit.

"Are you all right, Minty?" asked Uncle Drac. "You look rather flushed."

Nurse Watkins seemed annoyed. I expect she had been looking forward to a ride in an ambulance with flashing lights and sirens. "Huh," she said. "It was nothing more than a frog in her throat."

"A *frog?*" gasped Barry. "I knew it. I *knew* it."

Nurse Watkins gave Barry a withering

look. Then she turned her attention to Uncle Drac. "Well, Drac," she said. "You can certainly move when you want to. Let's do that again, shall we? *Left* foot up and lift and step. *Right* foot up and lift and step. *Knees!*" Uncle Drac scuttled off with Nurse Watkins in hot pursuit.

After that everyone except Wanda disappeared. You would think they might have been a bit more caring about the state of my health, but no.

Wanda was poking her shoe against the monster chair's great big claws. "What did you do *that* for?" she asked.

"It was all part of my plan," I croaked pathetically, and coughed a bit more.

"What plan?" asked Wanda suspiciously.

"To get Barry's frogs back. Can't speak any

more . . . must have a drink."

Wanda sighed. "What do you want?"

"I'll have a Coke. Oh, and two bags of cheese and onion chips."

~3~

BOIL IN THE BAG

"It's obvious when you think about it," I told Wanda after I had drunk the Coke and started on my second bag of chips.

"Can I have a chip?" asked Wanda.

"Okay, but don't eat them all," I told her.

"Not much chance of that," Wanda muttered as she took the biggest chip out of the packet.

Have you ever had a packet of chips where

there was one enormous chip in it and just a few really tiny ones—as if a cannibal chip had eaten up all the others while it was hanging around on the shelf waiting to be bought? Well, the crisp that Wanda took was one of those, so all I had left were the few scared baby chips. I tipped the rest of those into my mouth and then I said, "In fact it is so obvious I am amazed I did not think of it before."

"Whaaarsobvious?" asked Wanda, spraying me with chip bits.

"Yuck, Wanda. When did Barry's frogs disappear?"

Wanda swallowed and the cannibal chip met its doom. "Dad hasn't seen them for three whole days now."

"And how long has Nurse Watkins been coming to shout at Uncle Drac?"

Wanda counted up on her fingers. "Three days?" she asked. Wanda is not as good at math as I am.

"*Precisely*, my dear Wanda," I said, smiling like one of those detectives who has just tripped up a particularly difficult suspect with a clever ploy.

"Why are you looking like that?" asked Wanda. "Stop it, Araminta. It's scary."

I sighed. It is tough having a dim-witted sidekick, but I guess it is good practice—in case I ever get to be a real detective, which is one of the career options I have recently been considering. "Barry's frogs have been missing for three days," I told her. "Nurse Watkins has been coming here for three days. Two and two make four. Obvious, isn't it?"

Wanda looked puzzled. "But it's three," she

said. "And that makes *six*."

"No, Wanda, listen. Frogs gone: three days. Nurse Watkins here: three days. *Get it?*"

Finally Wanda got it. Her eyes opened really wide and so did her mouth. Which was not nice as I could see bits of chip stuck on her tongue. "You mean Nurse Watkins has Dad's frogs?" she said.

"Shh!" I pointed frantically behind her.

"Oh," said Wanda. "Er, good morning, Nurse Watkins."

"Good morning, dear." Nurse Watkins strode up to the monster chair and hauled her great big black nurse's bag out from underneath it. "I'll let myself out," she said. Then she zoomed across the hall and slammed the front door behind her.

"Shoot!" I said. "I wanted to look in her bag."

Wanda looked shocked. "You can't go looking in other people's bags," she said.

"You can if you are searching for evidence . . . or *frogs*."

Wanda gasped. "Frogs! You don't think she's got Dad's frogs in her *bag*!"

"She might. It is a possibility. We will just have to find out, won't we? Come on, Wanda."

Wanda can be quite quick when she wants to be. She jumped up and grabbed hold of my arm and in a moment we were outside on the front path. "If we hurry we could catch up with her," she said. "Then we could grab her bag and rescue Dad's frogs."

I followed her down the winding path to the rusty old gate, which had fallen off its hinges and was propped up by the hedge as usual. Something else was propped up by the hedge, too—Uncle Drac. Actually Uncle Drac was *in* the hedge. Spookie House is surrounded by tall, thick hedges that are great for hiding in. Uncle Drac has a really good hideout by the front gate where he can keep an eye on things—and do his knitting in the dim green light.

"Minty," he hissed, "has she gone?"

I could see the square figure of Nurse Watkins perched on top of her big black bicycle wobbling up the road. We would have to hurry. "Yes, she has. We've got to go, Uncle Drac. See you later!"

Uncle Drac waved his knitting at me. It was a very weird red and black stripy thing with lots of tendrils hanging off it. "Do you like your hat, Minty?" he asked.

"My *hat?*"

"Yes. I think it will really suit you."

"Oh. Uh, it's um . . . *beautiful*, Uncle Drac."

"Why don't you try it on?"

"No! I mean, no thank you, Uncle Drac. We've got to go. Byeeee!"

But by the time we had escaped from Uncle Drac, Nurse Watkins had disappeared.

"She's gone," said Wanda, staring at the bend at the end of the road. But I knew that even if a suspect is out of sight, you don't give up. All detectives lose their suspects at least once. You just have to find them again—and fast.

"Just around the bend," I said. "Come on, Wanda. If we hurry we can catch her."

Wanda looked worried. "It's out of sight of

the house. We ought to tell Mom where we're going," she said.

"She won't mind," I said.

"She *will* if I don't tell her first."

I sighed. Most detectives do not have to put up with their dim-witted sidekick having to tell her mother where she is going. "Well, go and do it then, but get your skates on, otherwise we'll never find those frogs."

Sometimes Wanda surprises me and I realize she is not totally dumb. This was one of those times. Wanda was really quick, and when she came back she really did have her skates on—*and* she was carrying mine. Wanda is quite good at skating. She jumped down the crumbly old steps by the front door, glided along the path, and handed me my skates.

"Now you get *your* skates on." She grinned.

I didn't need telling twice. I really love my skates. I am so glad that Brenda and Barry gave us both roller skates for Christmas, even though Aunt Tabby disapproved.

The road from Spookie House is a great road to skate along. It is very smooth and no cars come down there because of the notice Aunt Tabby has put up that says:

DANGER, UNEXPLODED MINES.

Wanda and I whizzed
along at top

speed, and very soon we had rounded the bend at the end and were zooming down the hill toward a small cottage by a stream. Suddenly Wanda did a show-off stop—the kind where you turn at the same time and end up facing the other way. I bumped straight into her and fell into the ditch.

It was not funny and I do not know why

Wanda would not stop laughing. I got out of the ditch—which luckily was not very full of water—and told her to be quiet or she would alert the suspect; then we would never find the frogs and it would be *all her fault*. My dim-witted sidekick stopped laughing and said, "There's her bike!"

Wanda was learning fast. Sure enough, there was Nurse Watkins's bike, propped up outside the cottage.

"Aha," I said. "We will have to stake out the cottage."

"What?"

I sighed. "We'll have to wait outside until she comes out," I said, which somehow sounded much less exciting.

So Wanda and I skated down to the cottage very quietly and hid behind the fence. Wanda found a small hole and peered through. "As I am chief detective *I* should do that," I told her.

But Wanda would not budge. "*I* found the hole," she said, "and they are *my* dad's frogs." She kept looking through the hole as though she was watching something extremely interesting, which I knew she wasn't as she was fidgeting a lot. After a while Wanda got bored and then the chief detective took over—just in time.

The cottage door creaked open and I saw a sweet-looking old lady with a bandage around her neck showing Nurse Watkins out.

"I'll see you tomorrow," Nurse Watkins's voice boomed.

"Will you?" The old lady sounded worried.

"Yes," Nurse Watkins told her very firmly. "I can fit you in at the same time as today.

After Mr. Spookie and before the mushroom farm." The old lady slammed the door and Nurse Watkins clomped off down the path. She put her bag into her bicycle basket and then stopped for a moment. She opened the bag and rummaged inside. "Shoot!" I heard her say. "I'll forget my head next."

The next moment she was banging on the cottage door and the bag was just sitting there, all alone in the sunshine. A good detective does not waste an opportunity like that; I shot out from behind the fence and hurtled over to the bike. Unfortunately I forgot I was wearing my skates. It is not a good idea to grab onto a bicycle when your feet already have eight wheels underneath them—in my opinion it just adds extra wheels to the problem. But that is what I did. Nurse Watkins's

bike fell on top of me—and so did the con-
tents of the bag.

Yuck.

You do not want to know what was in that
bag.

~4~

FROG VAN

"**W**ell, I never thought Dad's frogs were in the bag anyway," Wanda said the next morning.

"You *did*."

"No I didn't. It was a stupid idea."

Wanda and I were getting ready to go to the beach. It was a really sunny day and usually I would have been excited because I like the sea now. I never used to go to the beach

when I lived with just Aunt Tabby and Uncle Drac. Aunt Tabby thought the sea was dangerous and Uncle Drac does not really like daylight, and he especially does not like being out in the sun.

But just then I did not want to go to the beach, as I was in a bad mood. I was in a bad mood because:

1. Yesterday, after her bicycle ambushed me, Nurse Watkins marched us back to Spookie House. She found Uncle Drac knitting in the hedge and made him walk up and down the path twenty times.

2. Which annoyed Uncle Drac.

3. When Barry asked how come we had broken Nurse Watkins's bicycle, Wanda had told him that I had been looking in Nurse Watkins's bag for his frogs.

4. Which annoyed Barry.

5. And Brenda.

6. And Aunt Tabby.

7. And *me*. Because it was not true, as I never got the chance. In fact I had been savagely attacked by Nurse Watkins's bag.

It was just *not fair*.

But no one cares what I think, so we were going to the beach whether I wanted to or not. Ever since Brenda told Aunt Tabby about lifeboats and rescue helicopters, Aunt Tabby has changed her mind about the sea being dangerous and now she really likes it. In fact, I think she secretly wants to be rescued by a helicopter. Actually, I wouldn't mind being rescued by a helicopter either. But not at the same time as Aunt Tabby.

"You will enjoy it when we get there,

Araminta," said Aunt Tabby. Huh. Aunt Tabby always acts like she knows the future, but she doesn't.

"How can you know that I will enjoy it?" I asked. "I might get eaten by a shark. I wouldn't enjoy *that*."

Aunt Tabby raised her eyes up like she was looking for something in her eyebrows and sighed. "I don't suppose the shark would either," she replied. Which I did not think was very nice.

I had been thinking about what Nurse Watkins had said to the little old lady and I realized I had another clue. I was hoping that if I was grumpy enough everyone else would go to the beach and leave me behind because I had a plan—I wanted to sneak off to the mushroom farm.

But it was no good, we were *all* going to the beach in Barry's van.

Except for Uncle Drac, of course.

And Barry, as he was still looking for his frogs. I told Barry that we were still looking for them too, and he said it was probably better that we didn't look anymore, all things considered. But what Barry did not understand was that a good detective never gives up. In fact, from what I have seen, the more people tell them to give up, the more determined they are to continue. As soon as the detective's boss tells her that she is being taken off the case, you know that's it—she will go right on and solve it.

But if I couldn't go to the mushroom farm, I knew someone who could. So while Brenda, Aunt Tabby, and Wanda were making the picnic and finding the beach towels, I went to find Sir Horace.

Sir Horace is one of the ghosts in Spookie House. The other ghost is a weedy boy called Edmund who likes Wanda very much, but he would be no good at finding frogs because he would be scared of them. But I knew Sir Horace would help.

When you first see Sir Horace you do not realize he is a ghost at all; you think he is just an old suit of armor. But inside the armor is the real ghost of Sir Horace Cuthbert Shirley George Harbinger. Sir Horace got to be a ghost after a fight with some nasty people called FitzMaurice who left him (and Edmund) to drown in a horrible grotto and then took over his castle. One of their descendants, Old Morris, still lives there, although the castle has almost disappeared, and now it is *the mushroom farm.*

First of all I had to find Sir Horace. Sometimes he is easy to find, as often he just hangs around the hall. Sir Horace likes company and you can usually find him propped up beside the old clock watching the comings and goings. But that day there was no sign of him anywhere. I really hoped that I was not going to have to go and find him in his secret room, as that takes forever, and I did not want Aunt Tabby coming to look for me.

The other place Sir Horace hangs out is up on the landing. He does this when he wants to go to sleep or if he is in a bad mood. I ran up the big staircase from the hall and crept along the landing, which is really wide and has banisters so thick that you can swing from them—if you don't mind hundreds of spiders joining in too. I was very quiet; I did not want Sir Horace to hear me coming, as he can be quite good at hiding from me. It was almost dark on the landing because Aunt Tabby had closed all the curtains to stop the sun from coming in, and the brown paintwork kind of sucked up any light that was left. I couldn't see Sir Horace anywhere so I stopped and listened, and sure enough, I soon heard a telltale squeak of something that needed oiling.

I tiptoed along the dusty old carpet and soon saw what I was looking for—two pointy armored feet sticking out from underneath a long and suspiciously lumpy tapestry that hung on the wall.

"Boo!" I said, and pulled back the tapestry. Sir Horace jumped and his armor squeaked

like a scared hamster. Well, like quite a lot of scared hamsters, actually.

"Hello, Sir Horace," I said, as I got the impression Sir Horace was still trying to pretend he was not there. "Would you like to come out today?"

"**No,**" said Sir Horace in his low, booming voice, which always gives me goose bumps when I first hear it.

"Please," I said. "I need your help."

I thought I heard Sir Horace sigh. You see, because he is a knight he cannot refuse to help any damsel in distress. I may not look much like a damsel, but as far as the average knight is concerned, that is what I am. Also I was in distress. Well, sort of. On behalf of the frogs.

"**What can I do to help you, Miss Spookie?**" asked Sir Horace. He did not sound as keen as I would have liked but that did not matter.

"I want you to come to the mushroom farm. You know—your old castle where Morris FitzMaurice lives."

"Do not mention that name here, Miss Spookie," Sir Horace boomed.

"I want you to search the mushroom farm for frogs and report back to me—got that?"

"Frogs?" asked Sir Horace.

"That's right. Acrobatic frogs. Five of them."

"Oh."

I waited for Sir Horace to say something more but he didn't.

"Come on then, Sir Horace."

"What, *now*?"

"Yes. In fact we're late as it is."

"Can't it wait?"

"No."

Sir Horace gave a really big sigh. **"Very well then. I shall be with you in a moment, Miss Spookie. But if I am to return to my castle there is something I wish to get."** He bowed, then lurched to one side, threw his left leg forward, and set off along the corridor doing the weirdest walk I had ever seen him do.

Sir Horace has a habit of falling to pieces every now and then. Wanda and I always have the job of putting him back together again, but we never seem to get all the pieces in exactly the same place as before. So every time he gets rebuilt, Sir Horace walks in a different way. I guessed his weird walk might have had something to do with the fact that we last put Sir Horace together at the same time we were mending Wanda's bicycle. I had a feeling that some of the parts got mixed up.

I found Sir Horace waiting for me in the hall a few minutes later and we got to the van just in time. Wanda, Aunt Tabby, and Brenda had finished loading up with the picnic basket, rugs, beach umbrellas, windbreaks, air matress, snorkels, flippers, and all the hundreds of things that Brenda always takes to the beach. Brenda was sitting nervously in the driver's seat—because Aunt Tabby is teaching her to drive—and Wanda was already in the back of the van with all the stuff.

Sir Horace was on the doorstep staring at Barry's van. I was not surprised, as most people stare at Barry's van. It is very embarrassing, especially when you are in it. Barry recently painted his van (which used to belong to Uncle Drac) with pictures of his frogs. They were leapfrogging all over it, they had big scary eyes, and since he had run out of green paint, they were all weird colors. Also the paint had run. It was meant to be an advertisement for his troupe of frogs, which Barry thought would make his fortune, but personally I thought it would put people off.

"Hurry up, Sir Horace," I said. "Brenda's driving and she is likely to take off at any moment." Brenda does not have what Aunt Tabby calls "good clutch control," which is a fancy way of saying that when Brenda drives, the van leapfrogs like a giant frog itself.

Sir Horace clattered down the steps and I was glad that Aunt Tabby was so busy telling Brenda to remember to *let go of the handbrake this time* that she did not notice. Aunt Tabby has a policy of never letting you do anything that you want to, and I was pretty sure this would cover taking Sir Horace to the mushroom farm in the back of the van.

Wanda, however, did notice. But luckily, just as she shouted, "No, Araminta, I will *not* move over for Sir Horace," her voice was drowned out by the metallic screeching of Brenda crashing the gears and Aunt Tabby yelling, "Clutch, Brenda! *Clutch!*"

I pulled Sir Horace inside and slammed the door just in time. Then we kangaroo-hopped down the drive and out into the lane. It was a lovely sunny day, and as we passed the DANGER, UNEXPLODED MINES sign I smiled. Chief Detective Spookie was on the case.

~5~

FROG BUCKET

It is amazing that only one of us fell to pieces on the way to the beach.

Wanda spent the whole time moaning that she was going to be sick and I bumped my head hundreds of times, but a good detective is always on duty and I made sure I kept looking out the window when we passed Old Morris's mushroom farm. It was a good thing I did because there were tons of clues just

hanging around outside, waiting for a good detective to find them.

First: There was Nurse Watkins's bike leaning against the gate.

Second: There was Old Morris. He was carrying a large red bucket that looked suspiciously like it was full of frogs. Okay, I couldn't actually see any frogs because at that very moment Brenda went around a corner on two wheels, Aunt Tabby screamed, and something rattly happened to Sir Horace.

Third: The sign outside the mushroom farm no longer said:

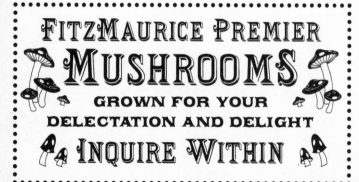

FITZMAURICE PREMIER
MUSHROOMS
GROWN FOR YOUR
DELECTATION AND DELIGHT
INQUIRE WITHIN

Now it said:

MORRIS'S WATER
WONDERLAND
**ANYTHING AQUATIC,
IT'S AUTOMATIC**
WE HAVE IT!!!!!

Fourth: Guess what the exclamation marks were? Yep, frogs—five jumping frogs. And how many frogs does Barry have? That's right. *Five.*

I was just about to explain all this to my sidekick—who was at the time underneath a pile of beach towels—when the van screeched to a halt and my sidekick landed on top of me. We had arrived at the beach parking lot.

Aunt Tabby threw open the door to the back of the van and peered in. She looked pale and her glasses were falling off her nose. She was not in a good mood.

"How on earth," she snapped, "did Sir Horace get in *here*?"

"Araminta *made* him get in," said Wanda. "He didn't want to."

"I did not," I said. "And yes he *did*. So there."

Wanda snorted in what she thought was a disdainful way but that only made her sound like a pig. You may wonder why Sir Horace did not say anything, but that was because due to Brenda's driving, his head had fallen off.

I fished his head out from underneath the beach umbrella and put it back on for him. I am quite good at putting Sir Horace's head on now; if you get it right it goes back with a little click. I listened for the click but nothing happened, so I just squashed it down a bit more and tightened up the bolts on his shoulders.

"Better now?" I asked him.

Sir Horace groaned. **"No,"** he said. **"Headache."**

"Let me do it," said Wanda, pushing in. Without even asking, she pulled Sir Horace's head off—which is very rude, as you should always ask someone first before you pull their head off. Then she put his head back and it went on with a little click. Huh.

"Better now?" asked Miss Smugpants.

"Perfect," said Sir Horace.

"Sir Horace will have to stay here," Aunt Tabby said, as she pulled out all the beach clutter from the back of the van. "He can't come to the beach."

"I have no desire whatsoever to venture onto the sands, Tabitha," boomed Sir Horace. "Rust is a terrible thing."

Aunt Tabby loaded Brenda and Wanda up with all the stuff and watched them stagger off to the beach. Then she slammed the van door shut. Sir Horace peered out of the window—how was he going to get out of the van now?

"Come on, Araminta," said Aunt Tabby briskly. "Leave Sir Horace in peace." She set off across the parking lot. "Come *on*, Araminta!"

I slowly followed Aunt Tabby, and when she had climbed down the steps onto the beach and taken her shoes off I suddenly said, "Oh shoot! I forgot my hanky, Aunt Tabby. I shall have to go back to the van and get it."

"No need, I've got some tissues," she said.

"But it's my special hanky," I said.

"What special hanky?" asked Aunt Tabby

suspiciously. "You don't have a special hanky, Araminta."

"I do. It's *so* special that you don't know about it."

Aunt Tabby sighed. "Well, hurry up then. And come straight over to the umbrella." She pointed to a large striped umbrella near the water, which seemed to have eaten Brenda and Wanda except for their legs.

I rushed back to the van and pulled open the doors. I don't think Sir Horace was that pleased to see me. In fact I think he was asleep.

"Come on, Sir Horace," I said. "I need your help. Remember?"

"**Oh. Ah.**" Sir Horace groaned. He heaved himself out of the van and very carefully stood up. As he did I heard something rattle inside him, all the way down from his head to his foot.

"Do you want me to get that out for you?" I asked Sir Horace.

"Get what out, Miss Spookie?"

"That rattly thing."

Sir Horace shook his right foot and it clattered like an old tin can tied to the back of a bike. **"No thank you, Miss Spookie,"** he said. **"I shall be needing it."**

I didn't get to ask him what it was, as a few little kids who had just got out of a car nearby had gathered around, staring and pointing, so I had to make my gibbering monster face at them. They ran off screaming.

Morris's Water Wonderland was not far from the beach. You just had to walk down a small sandy lane, but it was a long way for an old ghost in battered armor who was making an awful rattling noise. I wanted to make sure the old ghost got there all right, so I decided that Aunt Tabby would have to wait. "Come on, Sir Horace," I said. "I'll show you the way."

We set off noisily. Sir Horace made a loud clanking noise as he walked, and every time he kicked his left leg up he kicked up a shower of sand, too. It was *clank-clank thud, clank-clank thud*, and then *clank-clank thud* **ping**. I picked up a small spring that had shot off from somewhere and put it in my pocket. Nothing important fell off Sir Horace so I figured he didn't need it right then.

We were heading down the lane when I heard someone calling, "Araminta! *Araminta!*" It was Wanda, and she was as red as a beet from running.

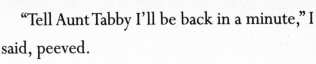

"Tell Aunt Tabby I'll be back in a minute," I said, peeved.

"Never mind Aunt Tabby," she said, puffing. "I want to know what you are doing with Sir Horace. You are up to something and you haven't told me. That's *not fair*."

"I have been following clues," I told her. "I am on the trail of Barry's frogs, unlike you, who seem to have forgotten all about them."

"I have *not*," said Wanda. "I am looking for them on the beach."

I sighed. "You won't find them there, Wanda. Nurse Watkins has frognapped them."

"No she hasn't. They weren't in her bag. The only thing you found in the bag was a—"

"Stoppit, Wanda. There is no need to remind me. Now look over there."

"Where?"

"The gate to the mushroom farm. What do you see outside?"

Wanda squinted. If you ask me she needs glasses. "A bike?"

"Not just any old bike, is it?"

"Isn't it?"

"It's Nurse Watkins's bike."

"Well, yes. But she said she was going there. We *know* that."

"But why is she going there, Wanda? What is her *motive*?"

"I dunno. Maybe Old Morris has a boil, too."

"Wanda, I told you not to remind me. . . . Anyway, I'll tell you why she is there. Because she is in league with old Morris."

Wanda gasped. "How do you know?"

"When you were snoozing underneath the beach towels I kept a lookout. That is why I am chief detective and you are not. You will see how I know in a minute."

We kept on walking—or lurching, in the case of Sir Horace—and soon we got to the gate. "Look at the sign, Wanda," I said, and I pointed to the five frog exclamation marks. Wanda gasped again.

Old Morris FitzMaurice, who is a thin, stringy man with a long greasy ponytail, had come into view—and he was still carrying the red bucket.

"What is it you wish me to do, Miss Spookie?" Sir Horace rattled. "Shall I cut his head off for you? Boil him in oil? Or merely take him prisoner?"

"Oh! Um, no thank you, Sir Horace. Although it is very nice of you to offer. I would just like you to rescue the frogs. I think they are in the bucket."

But Old Morris had seen us. "Hey!" he shouted. "What are you doing?"

He put down the bucket and stomped over. "Tickets go on sale this afternoon," he growled. "No unaccompanied kids and no scrap metal. You can come back then. Now stop staring at me like a couple of demented goldfish and scram."

I nodded and smiled. I was playing for time, which is a ploy that all detectives use when they are in a tight spot and the suspect looks threatening. Even though he was thin and stringy, close up he looked quite strong. Then I noticed his right big toe was bandaged and sticking out of his sandal.

"Do you play soccer?" I asked him politely. It is always a good idea to gain your suspect's trust and lull him into a false sense of security. Then eventually he will end up telling you everything you need to know, right down to why he did it and how sorry he is and what a great detective you are for finding him out.

"Are you trying to be funny or what?" he snapped. "Got bit by a turtle, if you really want to know."

I could see I was gaining his trust, so I went in with what is called a leading question. "Frogs can give you a nasty bite too, can't they?" I said, very sympathetically. "Are you sure it wasn't a frog?"

It was an important moment. I stared at Old Morris, waiting for the giveaway guilty look, but I couldn't see it. He had a strange expression on his face—it reminded me of the one Aunt Tabby has when she gets really upset but tries not to show it.

But I waited patiently and did not stop staring in case I missed a flicker of guilt. Old Morris was about to say something—and I was sure all would be revealed—when my dim-witted sidekick piped up, "What's in your bucket?"

Now that was really stupid. It gave the whole game away.

"None of your business," Old Morris growled. "If you want to see what's in the bucket you get your mom or dad or whoever is in this pile of junk here to buy a ticket this afternoon. Got that? Now *scram*. Pesky kids." He stomped back to the bucket—but Wanda beat him to it. Wanda can really scoot when she gets going. She zoomed past Old Morris and grabbed the bucket. "Hey!" he yelled.

"Frogs!" yelled Wanda, lifting off the lid.

"I *knew* it, they're in here. *I've found Dad's frogs!*"

Old Morris grabbed the bucket from Wanda. "Leave my bucket alone," he growled, "and get lost. If I ever see you kids around here again there will be trouble. Got that?"

But Wanda would not give up that easily. She grabbed the bucket back and hung on like a dog with a bone. I would not have been surprised if she had growled, too. A tug-of-war broke out between Wanda and Old Morris, but Wanda would not give. Old Morris was so busy fending her off that he did not notice the pile of junk moving in on him fast.

I did not know that Sir Horace could *run*. Without losing a single bolt he ran over and grabbed the bucket from them both.

"Who *is* that in there?" demanded Old Morris. "Come out and fight like a man. *Come on*." Old Morris, who was not as tall as Sir Horace, stood on tiptoe and peered into the visor. "It's no good hiding," he yelled.

"*I* am in here, FitzMaurice," Sir Horace's voice boomed out. It sounded really spooky. "I, Sir Horace, have come on a quest for frogs and to take back what is rightfully mine. Now stand aside and let me pass!" Sir Horace drew his sword—the one Wanda and I had given him for his five hundredth birthday—and pointed it at Old Morris. It looked really sharp.

"Careful!" I shouted. I did not want my suspect damaged.

"Do not fear, Miss Spookie. I have him at my mercy. I am in no danger." Sir Horace turned around and waggled his sword at me. "My trusty birthday present will protect me."

It obviously had been a long time since Sir

Horace had done any proper knight stuff and it showed. Even I know that you do not turn your back on someone like Old Morris for as much as one second.

In that second Old Morris had snatched Sir Horace's sword and thrown it to the ground. The next second he grabbed Sir Horace around the waist and threw him into a nearby wheelbarrow. Sir Horace landed with a horrible crash, and both his arms fell off. He lay in the wheelbarrow with his feet kicking like a stranded beetle. It was horrible. "Nora!" yelled Old Morris. *"Nora!"*

A little kid with carroty pigtails, grubby T-shirt and shorts, and long stick arms and legs appeared out of nowhere. "Yes, Dad?" she squeaked.

I was shocked. How could Old Morris

possibly be a dad? He looked ancient. And he was so *horrible*.

"Take the bucket, Nora," said Old Morris, "and get rid of those pesky kids."

"Okay, Dad," piped Nora. She gave Wanda a really mean stare and said, "Get lost, Wanda Wizzard, and take your googly-faced friend with you!"

Well. She could talk.

"Oh get lost yourself, Nora FitzMaurice," said Wanda haughtily. "We're going anyway. We don't want anything to do with your smelly old dump, *do* we, Araminta?" Wanda grabbed my arm and walked me away.

"But what about Sir Horace?" I hissed. "We can't leave him behind."

"We'll have to come back later," Wanda hissed back, "and rescue him *and* the frogs."

She pulled me across the lane to the sand dunes on the other side. "That Nora FitzMaurice is a real pest," she said. "She's in my class at school. She's really nosy. We don't stand a chance of rescuing Sir Horace or Dad's frogs if she's hanging around."

Aha. At last my sidekick was providing some useful information.

"We'll just have to come back in disguise," I said.

Then I raced Wanda to the top of the sand dune and pushed her down the other side.

SHARK!

As we slithered down the sand dunes in front of the Water Wonderland, Brenda, who has a kind of homing instinct where Wanda is concerned, suddenly appeared out of nowhere. There is no escaping Brenda once she wants you to do something, and Brenda wanted us underneath the beach umbrella *right now*.

And that is where we ended up—stuck

under the beach umbrella next to Pusskins, Brenda's cat, who was sitting in her pink cat carrier wearing a pair of sunglasses that matched Brenda's.

And if that wasn't bad enough, Aunt Tabby had brought my hat that Uncle Drac had knitted.

"Put this on, Araminta," she said. "It will

protect you from the sun."

"But it looks like a giant squid, Aunt Tabby," I said. "And it's made of wool. I'll *boil*."

"Better than getting sunburned, dear," said Aunt Tabby. She crammed the woolly squid onto my head and said, "There. It really suits you."

A weird snorting noise came from Wanda, but it soon stopped when Aunt Tabby got *her* hat out. You would not think that it was possible, but it was worse than mine. It looked like a green tea cozy with a pink fish on the top. And sticking down from the tea cozy part were two woolly blue braids.

"And *that* really suits *you*!" I spluttered. Then I had to hide under a towel to make myself stop laughing.

Even though we were wearing stupid hats

it didn't stop us from trying to get away from Aunt Tabby and Brenda, but it was no good. I think they had some kind of deal between them, because every time we tried to sneak off to rescue Sir Horace and the frogs, one of them was always there to jump out and catch us.

We nearly got away when Brenda went to get ice cream though. Aunt Tabby had been reading the usual kind of boring book she likes to read about fixing things—this one was all about wardrobes—how boring is *that*? Suddenly I noticed she was snoring. Aunt Tabby does not snore loudly, as that would be rude. Aunt Tabby tries to be polite, even in her sleep, but it was a definite snore. I nudged Wanda. "Let's go," I whispered.

But I had forgotten about Pusskins. As

soon as we stood up, Pusskins let out a loud yowl. Aunt Tabby sat up with a start and saw us creeping away.

"Are you going for a swim, Araminta?" she asked suspiciously.

"Er, yes, Aunt Tabby."

So we had to go for a swim.

The one good thing about swimming was we did not have to wear Uncle Drac's hats, because, as I pointed out to Aunt Tabby, they would only get wet and then they would fall off and sink. Which would have been a good idea, come to think of it.

It was quite fun in the sea really. I splashed Wanda and pretended to be a sea monster and then she tried to splash me but I was too fast for her and she got mad. Then she yelled, "Shark!"

Wanda has a very loud voice, and all the little kids who were busy jumping up and down in the waves screamed and ran for the beach. I grabbed hold of Wanda's arm. "You shouldn't do that," I told her. "It's not fair frightening the little ones like that."

"Let *go*!" Wanda yelled at me. She wriggled and tried to pull her arm away, but I can pull harder than Wanda, so I won.

Wanda was still yelling, "Let go of me, Araminta! *Let go!* There's a shark!"

Now I am not stupid—I know about sharks and stuff like that. I did a project on sharks once and I know that sharks do *not* live in the sea near Spookie House. They would not dare. But from the way Wanda was yelling you would think we were surrounded by sharks, and that that creepy music that always starts up when a shark circles someone was playing full blast.

It was only when Wanda inhaled a mouthful of water and had to stop yelling for a moment that I noticed how quiet it had become.

And how everyone was standing on the

beach pointing at us.

Then I noticed Aunt Tabby and Brenda pushing through the crowd and heading for the water waving their arms, and I wondered why since neither of them likes swimming.

And then I saw the shark fin.

It was really close. It didn't look like I

expected a shark fin to look somehow—it was much bigger—and all I could think was that if the fin was *that* big, then there must be an awful lot of shark attached to it.

Which was not a nice thought.

"Shark!" I yelled.

"I *know*," Wanda yelled.

Wanda has much shorter legs than I do and I usually beat her in any running competitions. But she won this one with miles to spare. I watched her shoot past me, her little legs churning up the water and kicking salty spray into my face. She did not even bother to look around to see whether I was being eaten by the shark or not—anyone would have thought that she did not care. By the time I had made it to the beach Wanda was sitting under the beach umbrella wrapped up in a towel and eating a cheese sandwich.

Aunt Tabby squashed me in a big bony hug while all the other people on the beach stared out to sea and watched the shark fin. They did not seem as excited as they had been when Wanda and I had been in the sea with the shark. In fact I thought they all seemed a bit disappointed, and I definitely heard one of the little kids say, "But, Mom, it's *not fair*. I always wanted to see someone eaten by a shark." And then his mother said, "Never mind, dear. Maybe next time." I do not know what small children today are coming to. Or their mothers.

There was no chance of us sneaking off after that. Brenda, Aunt Tabby, and Pusskins kept their beady eyes on us all afternoon. The beach got even more boring since the shark did not hang around for long after his lunch had disappeared. We all watched his fin swim off down the coast until it was out of sight behind the rocks, and then people began to pack up and leave as no one wanted to go in the water again. Soon we were the only ones left.

Aunt Tabby and Brenda started building a sand castle. "Come on, you two," said Brenda. "Help us fill the moat with water." But Wanda and I had more serious things to think about.

"I wonder what has happened to Sir Horace?" Wanda whispered when Aunt Tabby and Brenda were too busy trying to stop the bridge into the castle from falling down to eavesdrop on our conversation like they usually do.

"I don't know," I whispered back. "Old Morris has probably taken him to pieces by now and thrown him in the sea. Or sent him off to be recycled. Or melted him down. Or—"

"Stoppit, Araminta," hissed Wanda. "Stop!"

Brenda glanced up. "Are you girls fighting again?" she asked.

"No, Mom," said Wanda sulkily. "We're bored."

"How can you be bored on a beautiful day at the beach?" asked Brenda as she turned her bucket upside down and made another tower on the sand castle. "What more could you possibly want to do?"

Wanda did not say anything but I could tell that she was thinking. And then she said something brilliant. It was so brilliant that I am surprised I did not think of it first.

"We want to go to Water Wonderland," she said.

~7~
WATER WONDERLAND

Aunt Tabby does not approve of paying to see things that it is perfectly possible to see for free—like fish and turtles and frogs—and I was sure she would not approve of going to Water Wonderland. Which she didn't.

So I asked her when she had last seen a real fish—one that was swimming around and not just lying on her plate covered in bread crumbs. Aunt Tabby sniffed and said that that

was the way she preferred to see her fish, thank you very much.

That gave me an idea. You never know with Aunt Tabby—she likes eating really weird stuff. Who knows, maybe the frogs in Old Morris's bucket were not Barry's frogs but a coincidence—coincidences happen to detectives all the time and it is something you have to watch out for. Maybe what had really happened was that Aunt Tabby had snuck downstairs and fried up Barry's frogs as a midnight snack. I added the fried-frog theory to my list of possibilities.

"But what about *frogs* in bread crumbs, Aunt Tabby?" I asked.

As a detective you have to learn to notice when people look guilty. But Aunt Tabby looked like she normally does when I say stuff—kind of amazed and irritated at the same time—and said, "Don't be silly, Araminta." I decided to cross the fried-frog theory right off.

Then Aunt Tabby amazed *me*. She said, "Very well, we'll go to this Water Wonderland place if you really want to." I think the shark must have made Aunt Tabby go a bit peculiar.

Wanda and I had to wear our hats. I pointed out to Wanda that they were a really good disguise, as everyone would look at the hats and no one would notice who was stuck underneath them, not even Nosy Nora.

Before long before we were all at the ticket office in the old gatehouse to Water Wonderland with Aunt Tabby saying in a loud voice, "*How* much?"

The man selling the tickets was none other than Old Morris. His little beady eyes stared at Aunt Tabby and he growled, "You heard, lady. Take it or leave it."

"Leave it," snapped Aunt Tabby. "Rude man."

Wanda gave a mournful wail and Brenda—who was also being a bit peculiar since the shark incident—quickly opened the new bat purse that Uncle Drac had knitted for her. "Two adults and two children please," she said.

"All tickets cost the same," growled Old Morris. I looked at Old Morris carefully. He was soaking wet and was dripping water all over the tickets. I thought it was very suspicious. He saw me staring at him and stared back. Then he said, "Although I am considering charging more for kids since they are nothing but trouble."

I am sure I heard Aunt Tabby mutter "How true" under her breath.

Water Wonderland was packed. All the

people from the beach were there, which was strange as earlier the place had been totally empty. But I suppose the shark had scared them all so much that they only wanted to see safe fish.

Aunt Tabby looked around in disgust. "This is a *ghastly* place," she said. "I can't think why you want to come here, Wanda."

"Neither can I," I told Wanda. "It's horrible."

"Don't be silly, Araminta," hissed Wanda. "You *know* why we want to come here."

"I am laying a false trail," I hissed back. "I don't want Aunt Tabby getting suspicious." A good detective has to think ahead, but I do not know of any detectives who first have to get rid of their aunt and their sidekick's mother before they can go detecting. But *I* had to.

"Why don't you and Brenda go and have a cup of coffee?" I asked Aunt Tabby.

Aunt Tabby looked at me suspiciously. "Why?" she asked.

See what I mean?

The nearest mushroom shed had been turned into something called Squid Café. It was painted with a picture of a giant squid with its tentacles wrapped around a massive doughnut and a picture of an octopus drinking eight cups of coffee. Brenda was already on her way. Brenda's homing instinct for doughnuts runs a close second to the Wanda homing instinct.

Soon Brenda and Pusskins had sat down with three doughnuts and a milk shake; Aunt

Tabby was reluctantly sipping a cup of black coffee.

"Can Araminta and I go and see the fish, Mom?" Wanda asked.

Brenda nodded and shoveled another doughnut into her mouth.

"You've got sugar all over your nose, Brenda," said Aunt Tabby disapprovingly. She looked at her watch and said, "Don't be long. Fish Frolics—whatever *that* is—starts in half an hour."

So we had half an hour to find Sir Horace, rescue him, find the frogs, and rescue *them*. It was a tight schedule, but I knew Detective Spookie could do it.

Water Wonderland was a strange place. It was just a track with three long and very decrepit old mushroom sheds on one side of it and a scruffy green circus tent on the other side. Outside the tent there was a sign that said:

FISH FROLICS!
Fantastic Flying Frogs!
Fearless Fish and the
Surprise of Your Life!
Performance Starts
at 4 p.m. today!
Don't Delay!

"We've found the frogs!" said Wanda. "They're here!"

The next thing I knew she had wriggled underneath the canvas and disappeared inside the tent. I followed her.

It was weird inside the tent. It was filled

with a strange green light and smelled of a mixture of crushed grass and fish. There were three tiers of wooden benches arranged in front of a huge glass tank, which was full of water and a few bored fish. Around the edge of the tank was a wide wooden ledge with a ladder propped up against it and there was a big striped curtain hiding the back of the tank.

"I bet the frogs are behind that curtain," whispered Wanda. We climbed up the ladder, walked around the ledge, and peered behind the curtain. They weren't. There was nothing there—no frog bucket and no Sir Horace. Just a big empty ledge like a diving board and one lonely hat stand.

"This is a weird place," whispered Wanda. "I prefer mushrooms."

But there weren't any mush in Water Wonderland.

Now we checked out the ol shed opposite the tent. It had weird fish painted on the side a

had written "~~Akwarium~~ Aquarium" across the corrugated iron roof. A little kid and a big kid were coming out with their parents, and the little one was saying, "But *why* were the fish floating upside down, Dad?" and his dad said, "I expect they were just a bit tired." Then the big kid said, "Just a bit *dead* you mean," and the little kid burst into tears.

We peered into the ~~Akwarium~~ Aquarium but there was no sign of Sir Horace or the frogs. There was just a great big dripping tank lit with a few dim light bulbs swinging from frayed wires. The tank was green and very murky. The only fish I could see were a few yucky suckerfish with their heads stuck to the glass—and even those were upside down.

The next shed had pictures of turtles all over it—at least I think that was what they were meant to be, although Wanda thought they were rocks with legs. It was quite dark inside as only one light bulb was working; all we could see were old mushroom boxes and a few of Uncle Drac's bat poo sacks—which was why all the kids in there were holding their noses. In the middle of the floor there was a small dirty yellow plastic pool, and a few people were standing around it. Since Wanda and I were on important business we pushed our way through to check it out.

It wasn't worth it.

One small turtle sat on an upturned bucket in the middle of the pool. Personally I do not see the point in staring at turtles but there were a lot of people there who obviously did. The turtle stared at them and they stared at the turtle. Fun.

We left them to it.

Outside the turtle shed I found our first clue. I picked it up and showed it to Wanda. "Look!" I said. "A clue!"

"No it's not, it's a rusty old bolt," she said.

"Exactly. From Sir Horace's helmet."

"You don't know that."

"I *do*. When you've fixed Sir Horace's helmet as many times as I have you know every single bolt."

And then we found another one. And a bit further along the track we found another.

"Maybe you're right," said Wanda.

"I know I'm right," I said. "We are on a trail now. All we have to do is follow the bolts and we will find Sir Horace."

The trail led us away from the mushroom sheds, past a smelly old pond to the back of the mushroom farm. Suddenly I guessed where it was going. "It leads to the old ruins," I told Wanda. I felt really excited and just like a real detective.

"What old ruins?" she asked.

This is why Wanda Wizzard will never make chief detective. She does not look properly. The old ruins were staring us in the face. I very helpfully pointed them out to my side-kick, who was not appreciative. "That's just a pile of boring old rocks," she said.

But when I showed her the old door with Sir Horace's crest on it she changed her mind.

OLD RUINS

I could see why Wanda thought the old ruins were just a pile of old stones because that's exactly what they looked like, but of course I wasn't going to tell her that. The only reason that I knew they weren't a pile of stones was because once, as a special treat on Halloween, Uncle Drac had let me come with him when he delivered the bat poo to the mushroom farm.

Uncle Drac used to sell organic bat poo but he lost a lot of customers because he would only deliver it at night. I think he scared people too, although I don't know why, because Uncle Drac is the sweetest person you could ever wish to meet. But the night that I helped Uncle Drac deliver the bat poo Uncle Drac really scared Old Morris because he and I were both wearing our vampire teeth and we had a lot of fake blood on as well. Old Morris yelled and ran away when he saw us. We waited forever in case he came back but he didn't, so we left the bat poo by the gate and then Uncle Drac whispered, "Would you like to see the old ruins, Minty? They are very spooky."

Well, of course I had said yes. Uncle Drac

was right, the ruins were extremely spooky—almost as spooky as Spookie House. It was as if all the knights and ladies and princesses and pages from hundreds of years ago were still floating around and had nothing better to do than stare at you. But I didn't tell Wanda that because I needed her help to lift up the heavy iron bar that someone had put across the door since Uncle Drac and I had been there. Although Wanda is small she is quite strong and together we managed to lift off the iron bar.

"It's a bit like a prison—or a dungeon," Wanda whispered as we crept inside.

"It's not a dungeon, silly," I told her. "*That* is underneath the ticket office—in the old gatehouse."

Uncle Drac had told me that the ruins were the keep, which is the little round part in the middle of a castle that you retreat to if your enemies have knocked down your walls and are swarming all over the place. I suppose the idea is you can keep safe there.

I switched on my flashlight and Wanda switched on hers because she is a copycat. We shone the light all around the keep and Wanda kept going "Ooh" and "Aah," as if she had seen something interesting. But it wasn't interesting; it was full of junk. Old Morris had put all the stuff from the mushroom sheds in there, and there was a huge pile of Uncle Drac's bat poo sacks piled up against the far wall. They were beginning to fall apart and the bat poo was falling out, which is why the place smelled so horrible. Personally I think old bat

poo smells more disgusting than new bat poo, and that is saying something.

Then Wanda screamed—right in my ear.

"Shh!" I said. What Wanda does not understand is that if you are a detective you can't go screaming all over the place. I mean, when did you last hear a detective scream?

"But something poked my leg," she hissed.

"*What* poked your leg?"

"I don't *know*," wailed Wanda.

"Shh! Well, have a look and see."

"I don't want to, it might be *horrible*," Wanda whispered.

"I'll look then." I swung my flashlight around, and there it was. "Great!" I said. "You just walked into Sir Horace's wheelbarrow."

Sir Horace did not look happy in his wheelbarrow. His arms were jammed in along the

sides and his top half had come away from his bottom half.

"Sir Horace, are you okay?" I asked.

He did not reply.

"Hello, Sir Horace," said Wanda. "We've come to rescue you." But there was still no reply.

It was most odd because Sir Horace is a well-mannered ghost, which is why Aunt Tabby likes him, and he would never ignore you like that, even when he was in pieces. Something was wrong.

"Something has happened to him," whispered Wanda. "Something *horrible*."

I flipped open Sir Horace's visor and looked inside. It felt a bit rude really, like looking inside someone's head.

"Is he there?" whispered Wanda anxiously.

"I don't know," I said. "I'm not sure how you can tell."

"Why did you look then?" Wanda said grumpily. But all the same she peered inside too. "He's not there," she said, sounding very sure.

The thing is that Sir Horace is not the kind of ghost you can see, not like his page, Edmund, who is a weird sickly-green color and shimmers in an irritating way. Sir Horace lives inside his armor and that is all you see of him, just his shell.

"He can't not be there," I said. "That's where he lives."

"Not anymore, it isn't," said Wanda. "Maybe he's gone to live somewhere else."

"Don't be dumb, Wanda. Where would he go? Come on, let's get him out of here."

I picked up the wheelbarrow handles. Sir Horace was surprisingly heavy. "Oof," I said, "push the door open, Wanda."

"But Nosy Nora will see us," said Wanda.

"Nosy Nora won't see anything," I told her. "We'll take Sir Horace across the field and tip him into the ditch by the road. We can cover him up with leaves and stuff and no one will see him. Then we can come back later and pick him up in the van."

"You can't put Sir Horace in a *ditch*," exclaimed Wanda.

"Well, it's better than him being stuck in the keep. And it won't be for long, will it?"

Wanda sighed but she opened the door, and I wheeled Sir Horace out.

The sun seemed really bright after our being in such a gloomy place, and I was really happy to be back outside.

"Can you see Nosy Nora?" whispered Wanda, her little eyes blinking in the sunshine.

"Of course not," I said. "I told you it would be all right."

But it wasn't.

Nora FitzMaurice jumped out from behind a rock and screeched, "Hey! What are you doing with my dad's new suit of armor? I'm going to tell on you!" Then she shot off, her pigtails flying, yelling, "I'm going to tell on you!"

"Quick!" I said. "Let's get Sir Horace over to the ditch."

Together we ran across the field with Sir Horace rattling in the wheelbarrow as we bumped over the grass. We pushed through the hedge to the roadside and threw Sir

Horace into the ditch.

SPLASH!

It was a pity that the ditch was full of water, but I figured it was better than being old Morris's prisoner any day.

"We'll dry him out later," I told Wanda. "Now all we have to do is rescue the frogs."

~9~

IN CHARGE

I decided that we should walk back into Water Wonderland through the front gate, as Nosy Nora would not expect that. It was very quiet at the gate, with just a few bored-looking people lining up to get tickets.

Wanda hung back. "They'll see us," she whispered.

"Who will?"

"Whoever's in the ticket office."

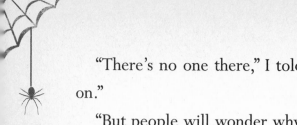

"There's no one there," I told her. "Come on."

"But people will wonder why we're walking in without buying a ticket."

"So what? They won't say anything. They'll think we belong here. We'll just hold our heads up and march right past them." Which is what we did. And then I had a great idea. A good detective does not waste an opportunity to search a suspect's premises, and this was too good to miss. I pulled Wanda into the ticket office.

"Araminta, what are you *doing?*" she wailed.

"About time, too," said the man at the front of the line. He had a baby strapped to his chest and a small kid hanging on to his leg, wiping her lollipop on his trousers. He did not look happy. "We want to buy some tickets. We've been waiting for hours."

"What?" I said.

"Two adults and two children *please*," snapped the man with the baby stuck to him. He pointed to a disheveled-looking woman holding on to a buggy containing a chocolate-covered twin of the lollipop owner.

"We don't do children's tickets," I told him, "as children are just as much of a nuisance as adults. More in fact. That will be five tickets in all."

"Five?"

"Two adults, two kids, and one baby. Two and two and one make five. Where's the ticket roll, Wanda?"

Wanda was not being much help. She was just standing there doing her goldfish impression.

"You can't charge for a *baby*," the man said.

"Yes we can. Do you want to come in or not?"

"No," he snapped.

The next customers were two old ladies who were much more reasonable. Wanda stopped being a goldfish, found the ticket roll, and we sold them their tickets. Then one of them said, "Mabel and I just love your fish and squid hats. Do all the staff wear such wonderful hats?"

"Only the ones in charge," I told her. Wanda gasped and dropped the ticket roll.

"I do hope you have some for sale," the other old lady said. "Vera and I are great fish fans. We have been looking for hats like these for years."

"You can buy these if you want to," I told her. "They are limited edition sale samples."

"Really?" The old ladies looked thrilled. "How much?"

I told them the price and I heard Wanda gasp again.

"Stop it, Wanda," I said, "and give me your hat."

The two old ladies put on our crazy hats,

which really suited them. They went off looking extremely pleased.

"But we're not in disguise now," said Wanda.

I sighed. "Wanda Wizzard," I said, "just think about it. When Nosy Nora saw us with Sir Horace, what were we wearing?"

"The usual stuff," said Wanda, looking puzzled.

"The usual stuff and the *hats*. So what will she have noticed most—the usual stuff or the hats?"

"The hats?" asked Wanda.

"So what will she have told Old Morris to look out for?"

"The hats?"

"And what will she be looking out for?"

"The hats," muttered Wanda.

"But *who* will be wearing the hats?"

"The old ladies. Oh," said Wanda. "I *see*."

I was working very hard at training Wanda Wizzard to be an efficient sidekick, but as you can see it could be tough going sometimes.

We sold ten more tickets and put the money in the cash box. Then we had the place to ourselves. It was time to search the suspect's premises for the stolen property.

It was obvious, once you knew, that the ticket office was part of the old gatehouse. The little window that you sold the tickets through was where the gatekeeper must have sat and checked everyone out. I think the part where they poured boiling oil on anyone they didn't like was at the top where all the ivy was growing. Any other time I would have liked to climb up the little spiral steps and had a look to see if there were any pots of oil left, but we had frogs to find.

The ticket office was really small and it took about two seconds to figure out that the frog bucket was not there. But there was a little room behind the ticket office with some coats hanging in it that looked more promising—just the kind of place you would hide a bucket of frognapped frogs in fact. There was Nosy Nora's school coat, which is just like Wanda's, there was Old Morris's grubby overcoat, and then there was—a shark!

Someone had hung up a shark in the cloakroom!

Wanda, who is nosy—which I suppose can be a good thing if you are helping out a busy detective who does not have time to think of everything—poked at the shark. "It's a shark suit," she said. "Look!" She heaved it off the hook and the shark suit fell right on top of her.

"Der-*dum* . . . der-*dum*, I'm coming to get you!" said the Wanda-Shark. "Snap snap *snap!*"

"Sharks don't go snap," I told her. "Only crocodiles go snap. Take it off, Wanda."

Wanda wriggled out from underneath the

suit. She looked very excited and her hair was sticking up like it does in the morning. "I like being a detective," she said. "This is fun."

"An *assistant* detective," I corrected her.

"I think, Araminta," said Wanda rather pompously, "that I am a *real* detective now."

"I don't think so," I told her firmly. "You still have a lot of training to do."

"*You've* never done any training, so I don't see why *I* have to."

"Some people don't need to. Some people are just natural-born detectives, they can't help it."

"Well, since I have worked out a whole bunch of stuff about the shark, I think that makes me a real detective."

"What stuff?" I asked warily.

"For a start, that was not a real shark in the

sea, it was Old Morris in the shark suit."

"I was just about to say that."

"Oh, but you didn't say it, *did* you?" Wanda was getting irritating now. "And you didn't say *why* Old Morris swam around in a shark suit scaring everyone, did you?"

"I don't have to tell you *all* my theories," I said.

"So why did he then?"

I sighed. "That is one of the questions I want to ask Old Morris when we arrest him for frognapping."

"You don't have to ask him," said Miss Smugpants, "because I am going to tell you. He went swimming in a shark suit to scare everyone off the beach and into Water Wonderland. He scared us, and all those little kids, just so that he could sell lots of tickets

for people to come and watch Dad's frogs. He is not nice."

"He didn't scare *me*," I said. "You should get your facts right if you are trying to be a real detective."

"I *am* a real detective," said Wanda. "And I think that from now on I should be in charge."

"What?" I was shocked. It was mutiny.

Wanda folded her arms and looked like the parking lot attendant who gave Aunt Tabby a ticket last week: kind of smug and I've-got-you-ha-ha at the same time. "Look at the facts, Araminta," she said. "Have we rescued Dad's frogs? *No.* Have we rescued Sir Horace? *No*—"

This was too much. "That's *not true*," I told her. "We *did* find the frogs."

"But we didn't rescue them, did we?"

"No, but we will. And we *did* rescue Sir

Horace. He is quite safe in the ditch."

But Wanda was not going to give up—I could tell by the fiendish gleam in her eye, which reminded me of Aunt Tabby when she knows you have done something wrong and she goes on forever until she finds out what it is.

"We may have rescued his suit of armor," she said, "but Sir Horace is not inside it."

"You don't know that, you're just—what was *that*?"

"What?"

"Someone tapped me on the shoulder."

"It is no use trying to change the subject," said Wanda, and then she jumped. "Someone just tapped me on the shoulder too," she whispered.

It was very spooky. A ghostly breeze ruffled

past and suddenly it felt as though someone else was there in the little cloakroom, listening to us.

"Let's get out of here," whispered Wanda. "This place is *haunted*."

But after Wanda's takeover bid for the Spookie Detective Agency I was not going to let on I was spooked too.

"No, it's not," I told her.

"**Yes, it *is*,**" came a ghostly voice. "**Miss Spookie, Miss Wizzard, I require your assistance, if you would be so kind.**"

~10~

THE DUNGEON

"See, I *told* you Sir Horace was not inside his armor," was all Miss Know-it-all Smugpants had to say. If she had been a real detective she would have questioned Sir Horace about his motive for getting out of his armor in the first place. And about why he was haunting the gatehouse and not rescuing frogs like he was supposed to. I mean, what is the point of being a damsel in distress

if your knight goes off and just does his own thing?

So it was left to Chief Detective Spookie to question the suspect—I mean Sir Horace.

Sir Horace said he had come for his long-lost treasure, which was in the dungeon underneath the ticket office. "I always dreamed of the day I could retrieve what is rightfully mine," he said. "And when you asked me to go on your frog quest I knew it was my chance at last. Because, Miss Spookie, I need your assistance. The trapdoor is here, if you would care to accompany me."

I really like dungeons and I especially like long-lost treasure, so I lifted up the trapdoor and we peered down into the dark hole. Wanda shivered. It was really cold down there. I switched on my flashlight (all

detectives must carry a flashlight) and we saw some steps leading down to an earth floor and some slimy green walls. It looked great.

"Come on, Wanda," I said.

Wanda followed me down the steps and soon we were standing in a perfect little dungeon. The dungeon was empty apart from a very old shovel propped up against the wall.

Sir Horace's voice echoed around the little

dungeon and I got goose bumps. He sounded even more spooky down there.

"I see you have found my shovel," he said. **"It is exactly where I left it. Now, perhaps you could dig a hole just where Miss Wizzard is standing?"**

"Me? Dig?"

"That's what he said," said Wanda. "Dig."

Sometimes a chief detective has to get things done and this was one of them. So I stabbed at the earth with the shovel and got going.

"Not there," said Miss Picky, "*here*." And she jumped out of the way. "Where I was standing."

"How can I concentrate if you keep hopping about like a demented rabbit?" I asked her. "Digging for treasure is a skilled job, you know."

It was a tough job, but about ten minutes later the shovel hit something hard with a big *thud*. As I scraped the earth away, Sir Horace—who had kept so quiet that I began to wonder if he had floated off somewhere—suddenly shouted, **"I see it! My treasure chest!"**

Aha! Another success for the Spookie Detective Agency.

Wanda and I dragged the chest out of the hole. It was really heavy and was just how you would expect it to be—dark, thick wood with a domed top. It was covered in metal studs and had two big iron bands wrapped around it. In the middle was a great big brass keyhole.

Sir Horace was really thrilled. Even though you could not see him, you could tell that his voice had a smile in it. A big smile. **"My treasure, my treasure,"** he kept saying, over and over again.

"Open it, open it!" I said. After all, it's not every day you get to see treasure that has been buried for five hundred years.

"Oh," said Sir Horace, and I could tell he was not smiling anymore.

"What's the matter?" I asked him, but he didn't reply.

"He doesn't have the key," said Wanda. "That's what was rattling inside his armor."

"How do you know?" I asked her.

"Deduction," said Miss Smugpants.

"*What?*"

"It's what detectives do. They put two and two together and make four." Wanda looked at me in a Nurse Watkins kind of way when she said that, although I don't know why.

"Well, if you know so much about where the key is, you can go and get it," I told her. "*What's that?*"

Thump, thump, thump. There were footsteps up in the ticket office. Big, clompy footsteps.

"It's Old Morris," whispered Wanda.

"Shh . . ." I hissed. "It might not be Old Morris, it might be—"

"Nora, Nora . . . is that you?" Old Morris yelled grumpily. "I *told* you not to leave the door open. Anyone could have walked in. *Nora?*"

"We're trapped," whispered Wanda. She

looked really scared.

We listened to Old Morris's big boots clomping across the floor. The footsteps were right above us now and I knew that any minute he would find the open trapdoor.

And then he found it. Very suddenly. Extremely suddenly, in fact. One minute he was stomping around shouting and the next minute he was flat on his back on the dungeon floor staring up at Wanda and me. He looked a bit surprised.

"Well, hello, Old Morris," I said in a friendly way, as I did not want him to feel that he had intruded on anything—even though he had. There are some times when you just have to be polite and I figured this was one of them.

But Wanda is not polite like I am. "Let's get

out of here!" she yelled, and she was up the ladder in two seconds flat. I followed her— fast.

"My treasure," Sir Horace groaned. **"I have waited five hundred years to get my treasure back from the FitzMaurices. Five hundred years only to see it snatched from my grasp yet again. *Aaarrghhhooooh.*"**

"Now stop it, Sir Horace," I told him in my best Aunt Tabby voice. "Just stop it. It will be all right. I have a plan." Now it was Wanda's turn to groan, but I ignored it.

I slammed the trapdoor shut.

"Hey!" came a muffled yell from the dungeon.

"Help me shove the safe over the trapdoor so he can't get out," I said.

"You can't do that," said Wanda.

"Yes I can," I said. "We don't want him getting away with the treasure, do we?"

Wanda shook her head.

"Hey! Let me *out*!"

The safe was really heavy but we managed it. There was no way that Old Morris was going to get out of there in a hurry.

"Now look," I said. "The Fish Frolics Show is meant to start in a few minutes and if it doesn't everyone, including Nosy Nora, will start looking for Old Morris. It won't take them long to figure out where he is, not with all that yelling. Then they will find the treasure—which will belong to him since he owns this place—"

"No he doesn't," said Sir Horace. **"I do."**

"Well, *we* know that and *you* know that, Sir Horace, but no one else does. As I was saying, I have a plan that will mean we get the treasure *and* the frogs. Okay?"

"What plan?" asked Wanda suspiciously.

"*We* are going to do the Fish Frolics Show."

"*What?*"

"And Sir Horace is going to be Old Morris."

Wanda did her stranded goldfish imitation. "But . . . *how?*"

"He's going to wear the shark suit," I said.

Wanda opened her mouth but she didn't say anything. She didn't have to. I knew it was my most brilliant plan ever.

~11~

HAUNTED SHARK

I t is not easy getting an old ghost in a shark suit underneath the edge of a tent, but we did it.

We crept around the back of the mushroom sheds to get to the tent since I thought that people might notice a shark walking around. On the way I had told Sir Horace, "When someone with a really annoying squeaky voice calls you Dad, you have to pretend that is who

you are. You are Dad. Got that? And then you have to tell her that Wanda and I are running the show. Okay?"

Sir Horace did not say anything for a bit and then he said, "**Why?**"

"Because that is a really important part of my plan. Trust me."

Wanda snorted like a pig, but I ignored her as I was too busy pushing Sir Horace underneath the tent.

The tent was empty except for Nosy Nora, who was hanging around beside the big fish tank looking worried. Outside the crowd was getting impatient to come in—the Fish Frolics Show was already twenty minutes late. You could hear babies crying, children squealing, and people grumbling to each other. I gave Sir Horace a push and said, "Just go and stand by the fish tank. Remember you are called Dad. Okay?"

I think Sir Horace nodded but it was hard to tell. But as he floated off toward the fish tank Nosy Nora yelled, "Hey, Dad! Where have you *been*?"

"Come on, Wanda," I said. "Let's leave him to it. We've got to find Aunt Tabby and Brenda and sort *them* out now." And I pushed her back outside.

We found Aunt Tabby and Brenda in Squid Café talking with Vera and Mabel. Aunt Tabby was holding our hats and she looked really irritated. Vera and Mabel did not look happy.

Brenda zoomed in on Wanda. "Where have you been? You're covered in mud and spider-webs." I could see a handkerchief moment coming on. Sure enough, Brenda fished out a big pink hanky, spat on it, and started rubbing at Wanda's face.

"Mo-om," said Wanda in a muffled way, and wriggled out of Brenda's grasp. *"Don't."*

Wanda did not tell Brenda where we had been, which was good. I thought Wanda's training was going quite well, as when she had first come to Spookie House she used to tell Brenda everything we did, which had led to a lot of Aunt Tabby trouble.

However, I could see we were heading straight for Aunt Tabby trouble here. "Araminta," she said sternly. "I have bought your hats back. If you need extra spending money you should ask me. I can't believe how much you made Vera and Mabel pay for these."

"Oh, but we wanted to," said Vera—or was it Mabel?

"Oh yes, we really did," said Mabel—or was it Vera?

I got out my detective notebook. "I can take an order for more," I said.

"*No*, Araminta, you can't," said Aunt Tabby.

"Oh please," said Mabel—or was it Vera—"we would love to order some more."

"How many would you like?" I asked before Aunt Tabby could say anything.

"We'll have two of each," said Mabel/Vera.

"So that there's no fighting," giggled Vera/Mabel.

"I will give your order to our resident knitter," I told them. "It will be ready in two weeks."

"Araminta, really . . ." Aunt Tabby said very faintly. But she didn't say anything else.

Suddenly Nosy Nora's squeaky voice came

over the loudspeakers. "Ladies and gentlemen, please make your way to the Water Wonderland tent where the world-famous Fish Frolics Show is about to begin!" The loudspeaker did a horrible high-pitched squeak and everyone winced. Then we all heard Nora say, "What was that, Dad? I can't hear what you're saying. What? Are you *sure?*" There was a silence, then the loudspeaker came on again. "Um. Would Wanda Wizzard and Araminta Spookie please make their way to the big tent as soon as possible. Dad—are you *sure?*" Then there was a crackle and the loudspeaker went dead.

"We've got to go," I told Aunt Tabby. "They can't start without us. Come on, Wanda."

"You are not going anywhere without your hats," said Aunt Tabby. "At least then I can keep an eye on you. Put them on."

There was no time to waste arguing over hats. I stuffed my squid hat on and Wanda crammed on her fish hat and we zoomed off into the crowd.

Nosy Nora was not pleased to see us. "You keep getting me into trouble," she said. "Did you know there are two old ladies wearing hats just like yours? I chased them all the way to Squid Café and nearly got trapped by your creepy aunt."

"Really?" I said. "What a coincidence."

Nosy Nora looked at me like I was one of those horrible suckerfish stuck on the side of that tank. "Anyway," she said, "I don't know why Dad wants you to help," she said grumpily. "He's not thinking straight. He sounds like he's got a cold or something."

"I expect he thinks you can't do it all

on your own," I said.

"There's not exactly a lot to do anyway," said Nora sulkily. "It's only the stupid frogs and then Dad does the shark thing and splashes everyone and then they all go home."

"I'll do the frogs," Wanda piped up.

"Oh all right," said Nora. "They're nasty, slimy things anyway." She picked up the red frog bucket and handed it to Wanda. Wanda grabbed the bucket. "I've got the fro-ogs, I've got the fro-ogs!" she sang and did a weird Wanda-dance around in circles.

That was a mistake. She blew our cover. One thing a detective should never do is blow her cover. It leads to trouble.

Nosy Nora looked suspicious—very suspicious. "What's going on?' she asked.

"Don't ask me," said the shark, peering out

from behind the big striped curtain at the back of the tank.

"*Shh*," I told Sir Horace—but it was too late.

Nora stared at me. "I don't believe it *is* Dad under there," she said. "I've heard all about you, Araminta Spookie, and I think you are fibbing."

"But——" I said. I was going to tell her that I had never *said* it was Old Morris in the shark suit, but Nosy Nora wasn't listening.

"I think it's your creepy aunt in there. It's

just the kind of weird thing she'd do. I'm going to look!"

"No, its not Aunt—"

But it was too late. Nora unzipped the shark suit and went pale. "There's no one there!" she yelled. "It's haunted!"

"That's right," I told her since, whatever anyone may think, I do not tell fibs.

"Where's my dad?" she yelled. "What have you done with him?"

We didn't say anything.

"I'll find him! I'll find him and then you'll be sorry!" Nosy Nora raced over to the tent flaps and threw them open. An excited murmur went up from the people waiting to come in. "*You* do the show, you and your horrible spooky shark—since you're so *smart*!" Nora shouted and she disappeared into the crowd.

Before Wanda and I had time to think, everyone rushed in and started fighting over the best seats. Aunt Tabby and Brenda won, along with Mabel and Vera, who plonked themselves down right in front of the fish tank. That was bad enough, but I couldn't believe my eyes when right behind them I saw *Nurse Watkins and Uncle Drac*. How did they get there?

But I didn't have time to think about that for long. Soon everyone was sitting down and a horrible hush came over the tent. A whole forest of eyes stared at us like they expected us to do something.

"What are we going to *dooooo*?" wailed Wanda under her breath.

There was only one thing we could do— the all-new Spookie Shark Show.

~12~

THE SPOOKIE SHARK SHOW

The Spookie Shark Show was amazing. Everyone said that they had never seen anything like it.

Wanda got the spotlight working and the frogs opened the show. I could see why Barry was so upset about losing his frogs because they are very talented, particularly when you consider how stupid the average frog can be. Barry must have put in a lot of training

hours—almost as many as I had put in training Wanda to be a detective.

The frogs leapfrogged all the way around the fish tank as though they had been practicing for weeks. Wanda trained the spotlight on them and followed them perfectly. She even got clever and started changing the colors so that one minute the frogs were blue and the next they were bright red, then purple. I had watched Barry with his frogs tons of times so luckily I knew all the stuff they could do. They did:

* The Leaning Frog Tower
* The Triple-Frog Pogo Stick
* The Double-Frog Cartwheel
* The Four-Frog Catapult

It was just perfect—until they fell in the fish tank and Wanda had to go in and get them. But that was okay; everyone thought that that was part of the show. Wanda made a lot of fuss, but she caught all the frogs and threw them back into the bucket. Then, just to show that we had meant to do that, I held the bucket up and bowed. Everyone clapped so I bowed again.

Meanwhile Wanda was trying to get out of the fish tank, but she only has short little arms and she couldn't pull herself up. "Araminta," she spluttered, "help me get out." But I didn't think that was such a great idea as the crowd was enjoying it and I could tell it would be a really dramatic moment for the shark to come in. I rushed over to the striped curtain at the end of the tank where Sir Horace was waiting.

"Sir Horace!" I whispered. "It's time for your shark thingy. Jump in."

The shark didn't seem very keen. **"I'll get rusty,"** it said.

"No you won't. You're not wearing your armor—remember? And you've always wanted to learn to swim, haven't you?"

"Have I?"

"Yes, you have. Just think how useful it would have been. So now's your chance." And before he had time to think about it, I pushed him in. There was a huge splash and the shark landed in the tank. The audience screamed so

loud that my ears rang. Wanda screamed too, which was great because it made the show very exciting.

It was fantastic. It really looked as though Wanda was being chased by a shark. The trouble was that I had forgotten about Brenda. As soon as Brenda saw the shark she raced up and fished Wanda out with the frog net. The audience loved it.

Wanda sat on the edge of the tank coughing and spluttering and looking grumpy, but Brenda was really getting into it. The audience cheered and whistled and Brenda did a curtsey. And then she did another one. And another. Since Brenda was stealing the show I told Sir Horace, "You can come out now." He floated up out of the fish tank and stood on the ledge. Everyone screamed! Brenda's eyes nearly popped out of her head and she keeled over with a great big *thump*.

I never thought I would say that Nurse Watkins was useful—but she was. She rushed onto the stage with her little black nurse's bag (the one she had stolen the frogs in) and lifted Brenda's feet up above her head. It was very dramatic, and when Brenda woke up the crowd gave a huge cheer and Nurse Watkins took a bow as if she did that kind of thing every day. I suppose it reminded her of all the wrestling matches she had won.

People say that you have to leave a crowd wanting more, so I grabbed hold of Nosy Nora's megaphone and announced, "Ladies and gentlemen, the Spookie Shark Show is over."

A big disappointed "Aaaah" went up from the crowd, but I just kept going because that is what you do when you are running a really successful fish show.

"Please give a big hand for Barry Wizzard's frogs!" I said. Everyone clapped and whistled. "Also Wanda and Brenda Wizzard, Sir Horace the Shark, and last but not least, Nurse Watkins!"

Everyone cheered and cheered. I thought they would never stop. I waited for someone to thank me, which is what they should have done, but no one did, so I said, "And I am Araminta Spookie. This was the Spookie Shark Show. Thank you!"

People whistled and stamped and clapped and I took a bow. And then I took another.

And another. It was fantastic. I think I shall probably consider running fish shows as a serious career option from now on.

But the adulation of a crowd is a fickle thing. Soon everyone was trooping out of the tent, the adults moaning about the hard seats and the kids whining for ice cream.

And suddenly Aunt Tabby and Uncle Drac were looming over us.

Uncle Drac was smiling but Aunt Tabby was not. She had a big frown and her eyebrows met in the middle like two angry caterpillars. I could see a serious Aunt Tabby moment coming on so I got in first. "Aunt Tabby, you have to meet me and Wanda at the ticket office in ten minutes—it's *very* important," I told her. "And bring Barry's van."

"Araminta, you are *not* going anywhere—"

Aunt Tabby started, but we didn't hear the rest. I had the frog bucket in one hand and Wanda's wet paw in the other and we were off, heading for the ticket office.

~13~

TREASURE

Nosy Nora had got there before us. We found her trying to push the safe off the trapdoor. She looked up when we came in and said, "Oh, it's you, Wanda Wizzard, and your weirdo friend. I see you fell in, ha-ha. What have you done with my dad?"

"We haven't done anything with him," said Wanda.

Nosy Nora snorted. "Well, he didn't get

down there all on his own," she said.

"Yes he did," I told her. "And then we put the safe there. It is for his own good. In fact it is probably better if he stays there forever."

"Why?" asked Nora suspiciously.

"There's a very angry ghost who is after him. You dad has stolen his treasure and he wants it back."

"Oh, *ha-ha*." Nora snorted again. It was not a nice snort. Wanda's snorts sound like quite a sweet little pig, but Nora's was more like an evil-minded camel.

"Yes, *ghost*. The one that was in the haunted shark suit. Remember?"

Nora did not reply.

"He's really, *really* mad," said Wanda. "In fact he will be here in a few minutes and if your dad doesn't give him back his treasure chest he will be even *more* angry. He has a very sharp sword, you know."

Nora looked pale. "Does he?" she said.

"Yes. And he is really good at using it," I told her.

I could see that Nora did not like the sound of this. I was right. "If Dad gave him back his treasure, would he go away?" she asked.

"Probably. You can never tell with ghosts, but I expect he would. I mean, why would he want to stay in this dump?"

Nora nodded. I could tell that she thought Water Wonderland was a bit of a dump too. "Okay," she said. "You help me get Dad out and we'll give the treasure back."

"It's a deal," I said.

"Shake on it," said Nora. So we did.

The three of us pushed the safe off the

trapdoor and Old Morris was up the ladder like a rat up a drainpipe. He was not in a good mood.

"Right, you pesky, kids," he snarled. "You can make yourself useful and help me up with this chest. Then you can scram—got that?" Wanda and I nodded. We were humoring him. Sometimes detectives have to do that. Also we needed his help to get the chest up.

Old Morris shoved the chest through the trapdoor and then sat on it, looking puffed. "Right," he said. "You two with the ridiculous hats can get lost. And don't come back." Then he stood up and groaned while he held his back and said to Nosy Nora, "You wait here. I shall go and get a crowbar. We'll have this thing open in no time. Who knows, it may make our fortune." He chuckled as though he

had made a clever joke—which he had not.

"But it's not yours, Dad," said Nora. "It belongs to a fierce ghost."

"A really *horrible* ghost," put in Wanda, which I did not think was very fair to Sir Horace.

Old Morris snorted like a whole flock of evil-minded camels and said, "You kids heard what I said—scram," and then stomped off to get his crowbar.

"Quick," said Nora. "Take the chest before he gets back. And those slimy frogs too, then we won't have to do those stupid shows anymore."

The three of us managed to carry the chest outside, and just as we got out the door Aunt Tabby, Brenda, and Uncle Drac turned up in Barry's van. It was perfect timing. We heaved the chest into the back. Aunt Tabby poked her head out the window and asked, "Where did you get that, Araminta?"

"It belongs to Sir Horace," I said. "We are rescuing it for him. And we have Barry's frogs."

Aunt Tabby did not look as thrilled as I thought she might. "Hmm," she said. "Beryl says that they should probably stay here for a while."

"Beryl? Who's Beryl?" I asked.

"Beryl Watkins, dear. She was sitting next to us at the show."

"*Nurse* Watkins? But she stole them in the first place. Of *course* she thinks they should stay here."

Aunt Tabby tutted impatiently. "Really, Araminta, you do say the most ridiculous things. Beryl didn't steal the frogs. They jumped into her bag when she wasn't looking. She had a terrible shock when she arrived on her emergency call to Old Morris's turtle bite and she opened her bag. Beryl doesn't like frogs. Anyway, they all jumped out and headed straight for the pond. She says they were probably tadpoles in that pond and wanted to come back to spawn."

I would have liked to question Nurse Watkins myself, since I was not sure that Aunt Tabby was a reliable witness. But there was no time for that—I could see Old Morris coming out of one of his sheds with a huge crowbar in his hand. It was time to go.

I pushed Wanda and the frog bucket into the back of the van and slammed the door, but as we drove out of Water Wonderland Wanda

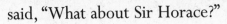

said, "What about Sir Horace?"

Wanda has a knack of reminding you of things when it is just a bit too late. I was about to bang on the little driver's window that looks into the back of the van and get Aunt Tabby to stop when I saw the weirdest thing.

Sir Horace—the suit of armor Sir Horace—was hitchhiking with his foot! Lying beside the ditch was the empty shark suit.

The van screeched to a halt and Aunt Tabby got out. A moment later the back doors opened and Aunt Tabby helped Sir Horace climb in. He looked really grumpy—you could tell by the way he plonked himself down right on top of his treasure chest and didn't say anything at all.

Aunt Tabby dropped Sir Horace's arms into the van with a clang and said, "Araminta,

I don't know how Sir Horace got into the ditch, or how his arms fell off, and I don't think I want to know either. But why do I think it has something to do with you? And as for how the shark suit got here. . . ." Aunt Tabby shook her head and slammed the doors shut.

I felt like saying that I didn't know why she thought it had anything to do with me either. But I didn't. Sometimes it is better not to argue with Aunt Tabby about things like that. Especially when she is almost right.

Sir Horace stayed grumpy all the way home. He sat on the treasure chest without even *noticing* it and did nothing but complain. He grumbled about his arms being on the wrong way, even though we put them back really carefully; he moaned about the mud and the leaves inside him; and he went on and on about rust. But at last I got my chance.

"Sir Horace," I said. "What are you sitting on?"

"Something rusty, I expect," he said gloomily. **"Just my luck. Rust is catching, you know."**

"We know," said Wanda grumpily.

And then Sir Horace's head drooped and he started snoring. And when Sir Horace snores, there is no way you can wake him up. You just have to stuff your fingers in your ears and sing very loudly to drown out the noise. Which is what Wanda and I did. All the way home.

"That was nice singing, dear," said Brenda as she let us out of the van. Brenda thinks everything that Wanda does is nice, unlike Aunt

Tabby, who thinks nothing I do is nice at all.

Aunt Tabby was not pleased about having to lift Sir Horace out of the van as well as his treasure chest, even though I told her how important it was. We propped Sir Horace up beside the big clock in the hall, and he suddenly woke up. The first thing he saw was the chest.

"My treasure!" he said, and his voice had a really happy sound to it. **"Miss Spookie, Miss Wizzard, you have been as good as your word. How could I ever have doubted you?"**

"The Spookie Detective Agency always keeps its word, Sir Horace," I said.

"You mean the Wizzard Detective agency," Wanda butted in.

"No I do not," I told her.

"Yes you do," said Wanda. "Who found the

frogs? Who solved the mystery of the shark? Who got Nosy Nora to let us have the treasure chest?"

"I did," I said.

"No you didn't—*I* did."

"May I suggest," boomed Sir Horace, who sounded much better now that he was back inside his armor, **"may I suggest a compromise. The Spookie-Wizzard Detective Agency has a very good sound to it."**

"Okay." I sighed an Aunt Tabby sigh. "The Spookie-Wizzard Detective Agency it is."

"Wizzard-Spookie Detective Agency sounds better," said Wanda.

"Sometimes," Sir Horace told her, **"it is best to stop while you are ahead. I would advise that at this particular moment, Miss Wizzard."**

"All right, Sir Horace." Wanda smiled. "Are

you going to open your treasure chest now?"

Sir Horace bent down with a horrible grinding noise, unscrewed his right foot, and took out a big brass key. Sir Horace keeps all

his keys in his feet. It's an odd place to keep keys, but I suppose he always knows where to find them.

The key turned easily and Sir Horace lifted up the lid. Wanda and I peered in; we were both really excited at the thought of seeing real buried treasure.

It was a big disappointment. It was nothing but moldy old papers, a battered whistle, and some funny little leather bags. It was very boring.

"Pooh," said Wanda, holding her nose. "It smells horrible."

It did. It smelled like a mixture of Brenda's gherkin soup and the cat's litter box. Not nice.

"Where's the treasure?" asked Wanda, who does not mind asking nosy questions, which I suppose will come in useful in the Spookie-Wizzard Detective Agency.

"***This* is my treasure**," boomed Sir Horace. "**All my precious letters and keepsakes. Even my lucky rabbit's foot.**" He bent down and lifted out a disgusting lump of fur.

"Eurgh," said Wanda. "That's what smells so horrible."

"What about the coins?" I asked.

"And the precious jewels?" said Wanda.

"And the silver plates?"

"And the doubloons?"

"The what, Wanda?"

"Doubloons. Old gold coins."

Sir Horace shook his head. **"Never had much in the way of that,"** he said, rummaging in the chest. **"Oh look, here's my old knight school report. . . ."**

We left him to it and went to find Barry. We still had a bucket of frogs to deliver.

We passed Uncle Drac on our way out. He was sitting in the broom cupboard in his favorite armchair with his feet up. He had already started on one of Mabel's—or was it Vera's?—hats. "Hello, Minty, hello, Wanda," he said. "It's nice to see you back. Oh, my feet are killing me but it was worth it. Ho-ho."

"What was worth it, Uncle Drac?" I asked him.

Uncle Drac chuckled. "I bet old Watkins that I could walk all the way to Old Morris's mushroom farm. She said she'd eat her hat if I could. But I did it. Ho-ho."

"Wow. How long did it take her, Uncle Drac?"

"How long did what take her, Minty?"

"To eat her hat."

Uncle Drac laughed. "I told her that I'd let her off if she told Tabby that I didn't need her anymore. Which she did. Spookie House is now a Nurse Watkins–free zone."

We left Uncle Drac knitting happily and went to find Barry.

Barry was wandering around the garden, poking under rocks with a stick in a miserable kind of way.

He looked up and saw us, and guess what he said? Yes, you're right. He said, "Araminta, *where* have you put my frogs?"

This was the moment I had been waiting for. "In the bucket," I said, and I handed him the red frog bucket.

Barry lifted off the lid a little suspiciously. I don't know what he expected to find in there. But when he saw his frogs he smiled a huge smile. And then do you know what he said? He said, "I *knew* you had them."

Well. That was all the thanks I got.

Wanda winked at me. "Come on, Araminta," she said, "they're only boring old frogs. Let's go and do something fun."

Sometimes Wanda can be really nice, like a real best friend.

Later that night, when we had used up all of Wanda's bike oil on Sir Horace getting him moving again, put his arms on properly, and cleaned off all the leaves and mud from the ditch, we were talking in bed in our Tuesday bedroom.

We were deciding what would be the next job for the Spookie-Wizzard Detective Agency, although now that I am going to run fish shows I must admit I was not quite so interested in the agency as I might have been. I was feeling tired and I leaned back on my pillow. There was something hard underneath it. I put my hand under the pillow to see what it was and pulled out a small leather pouch. It smelled of Brenda's pumpkin soup and the cat's litter box.

"Look what I've found!" I showed it to Wanda.

Wanda lifted up her pillow too. I really hoped there was something there for her as well. And there was—another little leather pouch that looked just the same. "What do you think it is?" she whispered.

"I don't know—open it and see," I said.

"No, you open yours and see."

"We'll both open them together, okay? One . . . two . . . three!" We tipped the pouches on top of our pillows.

"Wow," breathed Wanda. *"Look."* She held up a thick gold disc threaded onto a leather cord. It was just like mine.

"There's writing on it," I said.

"Oh yes." Wanda screwed her eyes up and squinted at the words.

"It's Sir Horace's funny spelling again," I told her. "*He* must have climbed all the way up the attic stairs and given us these. You did a good job with your bike oil, Wanda."

"For a . . . True and . . . Faithefull . . . Frende," said Wanda very slowly. "That's what it says."

And it did. It said that on mine, too. Which is not such a bad description of Wanda Wizzard, when you come to think of it. Or Sir Horace. Or me, I think.

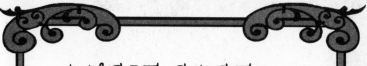

ANGIE SAGE, the celebrated author of the Septimus Heap series, shares her house with three ghosts who are quite shy. Two of the ghosts walk up and down the hall every now and then, while the other one sits and looks at the view out of the window. All three are just about the nicest ghosts you would ever wish to meet. She lives in England. You can visit her online at www.septimusheap.com.

JIMMY PICKERING studied animation and has worked for Hallmark, Disney, and Universal Studios. He is the illustrator of several picture books. You can visit him online at www.jimmypickering.com.

VISIT ARAMINTA ONLINE!

Go to www.harpercollinschildrens.com/aramintaspookie
to play games, send spookie e-cards, and learn more
about the kooky inhabitants of Spookie House.